19/12/2021

Dearest Fiora

Happy christmas!

I hope you enjoy this book, the original story was told by a man who used to live not far from me in crosley, his daughter has had them published for good children like you to enjoy reading.

Love & kisses

Moira Rose
xx

Brian Sears

Don't touch the Trifle Timothy Bear!

Illustrated by
Kim Gregory

It was the day before Teresa's birthday. Timothy had just watched mum make a special trifle for her party.

She had put fruit at the bottom, a layer of
sponge next, some jelly in the middle and

Pink blancmange

poured on the top.

Then mum put the trifle to set on
the top shelf of the fridge.
"It looks delicious"
Timothy said.

Then it was time for mum to take Teresa out shopping for a new party dress.

"We won't be long" mum said. "Help yourself to a drink and a biscuit but

"Don't touch the Trifle!"

Timothy hadn't been left on his
own indoors before. He went happily
upstairs to his room and started to play
with his Action Bear.

It wasn't long before Timothy tired of playing on his own and reckoned he was hungry. He went from his room on to the landing and, as he was on his own, he decided to slide down the bannister!

Wh-ee-ee-ee-ee

bump!

He landed on his bear bottom!

He went into the kitchen
and ate his biscuit.

It was easy to check that the
trifle was safe on its shelf...

...yes,
everything was in order.

"Don't touch the trifle Timothy Bear!"

Echoed his mum's voice
inside his head.

Back in his bedroom, his train set only kept his
interest for a while when he thought he felt thirsty.
Again he mounted the bannister.

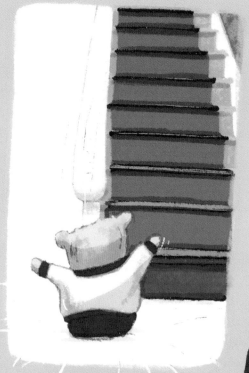

Wh-ee-ee-ee-ee **bump!**

Once more he was on his bear bottom!

This time he checked up on the trifle first. It seemed all right but perhaps he should take a closer look.

"Don't touch the Trifle Timothy Bear!"

Timothy dragged a stool to the fridge and climbed up. The stool was just the right height.

"Don't touch the Trifle Timothy Bear!"

His eyes were level with the trifle...

The jelly looked set but what about the blancmange?
Perhaps he should get the trifle on to the kitchen table
for closer inspection. Yes he'd do that. Mum had
said not to touch the trifle - it would be all right to
lift the bowl down wouldn't it? Timothy climbed
carefully down from the stool. He did wobble a bit
and the blancmange wobbled with him. It wasn't set
but the whole trifle looked fine on the table.

Unfortunately a plan was forming in Timothy's head.

It would need a spoon to put it into operation and
Timothy found one in the drawer.
He lifted out a spoonful of the blancmange.

The rest of the blancmange was still runny enough that it covered it back over. You couldn't tell there was a spoonful missing. Mum had said "Don't touch the trifle!"
But she would never know. So it wouldn't matter would it?

The blancmange was truly delicious.
And if it worked for one spoonful...

SURELY it would work for more.

Several

spoonfuls

later

the over-confident, careless Timothy dug his spoon into
the layer of jelly which certainly **was** set. None of the other
jelly came to fill up the jagged hole. Only a little pink
blancmange dribbled into the jelly crater.

Timothy felt miserable. Could he blame anyone else?
Could he make it all better again? He didn't even put
the trifle back on its shelf. He forgot all about having a drink.

He dawdled to the stairs and slowly started to mount them one by one. Even the bannister had lost its appeal.

Dismally he sat on his bed. It wasn't long before he heard the key unlocking the front door. Teresa's excited voice floated about the house. Then mum's stern voice. "Timothy!"

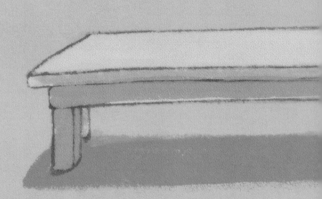

Timothy dragged himself back downstairs. Mum and
bear cub faced each other across the kitchen with the
evidence of what had been going on between them.

That story was clearly written on Timothy's sad face.
"Get straight to your room, get into bed and stay there
until dad comes home."

Although it was only four o'clock in the afternoon, that is what happened. It was a quiet house, even Teresa had lost her bounce. It was getting dark when Mr and Mrs Bear made their way to Timothy's room. Timothy had had time to sort himself out a bit.

I'm really, really sorry," he began as he poured
out how it had all happened.
"But how do we know you're really, really sorry?"
wondered dad.
A tear escaped from Timothy's eye and exploded
on the duvet to be followed by several more.

Dad nodded to mum.
"All right" said mum, "we can see you're really sorry,
I'll get you up early tomorrow and you can help me
make a new trifle."

Teresa, in the end, had a great birthday.
All her friends enjoyed the tea Mrs Bear had made for
them and the special trifle tasted as delicious as it had
looked. Oh yes, Timothy enjoyed it too...

... he was even allowed a second helping!

About The Author

Timothy Bear came into Brian's life when he was living in Bristol in 1974. He was helping at a camp for children from Muller's Children's Home. One young boy lost his teddy bear out of a car window on the way to the camp. Brian bought the boy a new teddy, and made up stories about him for the rest of the trip. That Christmas Brian was given a matching bear...

Timothy Bear!

Brian wrote and told stories about Timothy over the next 40 years, delighting the imaginations of children and adults in Croxley Green, Hertfordshire. As headteacher of Yorke Mead School, he often told Timothy Bear stories in the school assembly, as well as in local churches. Brian passed away in 2016 at the age of 73. His wife, Ros, daughters and grandchildren miss him very much, along with hundreds of "children" of all ages.

Printed in Great Britain
by Amazon